With special thanks to Susanna

Copyright © 2020 Glenn Sealey and Jeremy Love

All rights reserved. This book or any portion of thereof may not be reproduced or used in any manner whatsoever without the express written permission of the publisher, except for the use of brief quotations in a book review, for research or for private study.

At the bottom of a garden,

Under two cherry trees,

Lives a sad little monster,

And his loopy pet bee.

Now one day he heard the bell ring,

From his post box up above,

So Sid went way up to his hatch,

To find out what it was.

"Ding Ding!"

'A letter! It's a letter!'
He shouted down below,
And read the message word for word,
So proud he was to show.

'Hello, Hello.' The letter read,
'I'm coming soon to stay,
Better get the kettle on,
It won't be long. Love Dave.'

Hello hello.
I'm coming soon to stay.
Better get the kettle on,
It won't be long
Love Dave
x.

Our Sid he didn't know a Dave,
But his memory was not great.
A friend's a friend he did decide,
There is no time to wait.

So right away he got to work,
To welcome in his guest.
'I'll do the things to fix this place,
To make it look its best.'

'First of all he will need a place,
To get himself some sleep.'
And with an axe he halved his bed,
So Dave could count some sheep.

'Then what about some tasty grub,

He can't come here and starve.'

So he snuck out to the garden,

And plucked a sprout to carve.

'To wash himself I'll build a bath,

From wood and twigs and mud.'

Then he filled it with some water,

And watched his layer flood.

'Well now I think I'm ready,
To welcome in this Dave.'
Then sure enough he heard a knock,
From way above the cave.

Up he went to take a peek,
And what he saw was bad.
Dave his friend was at the door,
Of the house across the land.

'Blast those awful Johnsons!'
But sure enough he found,
The letter was addressed to them,
The name was clear and round.

And as he cried the comfort came,
From Bob the Bee his pal.
'Yes!' Sid said. 'My friend' he said,
'Some fun we'll have, we shall!'

So up they got and out they went,

To play out in the sun,

They found a hundred things to do,

And all with endless fun.

'Oh Bob you were here all along,
How could I be so rude!
Let's share the bed, let's have a bath,
Let's get stuck into the food.'

So nothing then was wasted,
Their new life there was set,
How could he only think of Bob,
As simply just his pet?

Now at the bottom of a garden,

Beside two cherry trees,

Lives a happy little monster,

And his friend called Bob the Bee.

And for some strange reason Sid and Bob never received
any more post...

Printed in Great Britain
by Amazon

15040318R00016